Shreds of thoughts II - Gedankenfetzen

Astrid Evelt

Shreds of thoughts II -
Gedankenfetzen

Bibliografische Information der Deutschen Nationalbibliothek:
Die Deutsche Nationalbibliothek verzeichnet diese Publikation in der Deutschen
Nationalbibliografie; detaillierte bibliografische Daten sind im Internet
über http://dnb.d-nb.de abrufbar

© 2013

Herstellung und Verlag: BoD - Books on Demand, Norderstedt

ISBN: 9783732279944

Vorwort oder so was

Ein weiteres Mal habe ich mich daran gesetzt ein Gedankenfetzen-Buch zu machen.
Ich weiß, dass man sich von kreativen Werken, insbesondere Songs, angesprochen fühlen kann. Ich bin ja kreativ unterwegs und da ich in meinen "Werken" auch mal das Wort "Du" benutze, auch wenn ich das allgemein meine, um meine Gefühle und Gedanken auszudrücken, kann man sich von den Sachen berührt fühlen.
Natürlich kann ein Kreativer auch immer jemand Bestimmten im Kopf haben, aber das muss nicht. Ich schreibe auch manchmal Dinge aus der Sicht eines anderen (wie ich reagieren würde, wenn ich die Person wäre) oder manchmal schreibe über das,
was ich von anderen mitkriege auf andere Weise, um damit umzugehen, aber ohne die Person verletzen zu wollen.

Man fühlt sich meist sofort angesprochen, besonders bei dem Wort "Du" und das passiert dann auch mal vielen Leuten und da kann es auch durchaus auch passieren das Leute sich vielleicht einen Schuh anziehen, der ihnen gar nicht gehört...
Also, wünsche ich euch gutes Durchkommen durch den Dschungel der Gedanken und Gefühle und verrennt euch nicht in irgend etwas, Astrid

PS. Wer Fehler findet, darf sie gerne behalten. Wenn man stundenlang an etwas arbeitet, passieren Fehler.

Ein aufbauender Gedanke:

Manchmal ist das Leben hart
und wir werden schwach

Du bist der klassische "Harte Schale -
Weicher Kern" - Typ;
jemand mit einer zerbrechlichen Seele,
die durch seine Kämpfernatur verdeckt wird

Für viele Leute bist du wie ein Fels in der Brandung
als Meister seines Fachs

Jemand, der Leuten mit richtigen Worten und Gesten
ein Stück weit auf ihren Weg bringt und begleitet

Du hast ein offenes Ohr und du gibst anderen die Ruhe,
Kraft und das Durchsetzungsvermögen weiterzugehen

Viele, die sich bei anderen wie Verlierer fühlen,
können in deiner Nähe die Gewinner sein

Und höchstwahrscheinlich bist du für so manchen
der Held seiner Träume

Hin und wieder wirst du zum Ritter der Herzen;
zum Kämpfer für Gerechtigkeit

Über dich wurde schon so manche Geschichte
erzählt und sogar zu Papier gebracht

Es ist nicht leicht als starker Mensch
jemanden zu finden, bei dem man
sich fallen lassen und auch mal
Schwächen zeigen kann

Aber auch das ist eine Stärke;
weiterzumachen bis
die richtige Person da ist, bei
der man so sein kann wie man ist

Du hast die Vitalität,
die Energie und du besitzt auch
das Durchhaltevermögen,
um deine Wünsche zu erreichen
und jemanden zu finden
und den Schatz zu zeigen, der in dir steckt

More strange thoughts:

I LOVE YOU – See, I wrote it down
More than that – I really mean it
And above all – I mean you, you fool

Does it shock you, when you read it?
Does it bug you?
Does it even reach you – in your brain
Or in your heart or both?

Is your mind reeling
Or is it ringing in your ears,
even if it's only written on paper?
It's deep down imprinted in my heart and soul

Do you feign ignorance?
That silly girl can't mean you – yes, you're right,
a silly girl does not mean you,
but this foolish woman does!

You read those lines and wonder, what's what
I cannot tell you, if you need to ask this

Sometimes I just write down things, feelings
and thoughts

Sometimes they reflect me, others or the situation
With no direct connection to a person

Sometimes they're just a statement
And you know, it's all up to you
What you make of this:

The rambling of a bloody dolt
The cries of a foolish, desperate woman
The reflection of me, others or the situation
The statement of a deep rooted feeling
That gets more tangible by saying
I love you, _____ !

Did you really expect me to write a name in this?
Did you really think, I'm that foolish?

I know what it means to me and who you are,
It's all up to you to find out what's what!

A touch of love?

Sometimes I wished I could really feel your love
But it never happened in that way
No touches, hugs, caresses and kisses to prove me
what I feel is not an illusion
Do you know how much I wanted to touch you,
kiss you, feel you when I first saw you?

I felt a spark of a sensation I never knew before
You were in front of me with that spark in your eyes,
Only a few steps for me to reach you
But I only managed a shy smile
I let the chance pass

I wished you had closed the gap between us
But you let the chance pass as well
I have no clue whether you wanted me or not,
but the chance is gone

Now I stand here without even so much as
an inkling about feeling love
I don't know, if we had a second chance
that I could create such feelings in me,
let alone in you in reality

A touch or a kiss would reassure me that
the passion is something we both could feel
and not a figment of my imagination

When I see you now, I still crave for your touch,
but if you would make a move on me now
I would only shy away from you

The fear of not being able to create those
wonderful sparks again and bring them into
reality only makes me somewhat numb and wary

Too many doubts in my mind create a much
bigger gap between us and it seems like a
mountain
Just a little kiss could break those walls around
my heart down, but that seems out of reach

The hope is still in me that things can change
for the better and it's all I have

Sonnenaufgang

Ein Sonnenaufgang ist etwas Herrliches
Sonnenstrahlen durchbrechen rosa Wolken,
langsam wird die Welt in warme Farben getaucht

Die Farbe malt Bilder an den Himmel,
bei denen man sich selbst im Asphaltdschungel
wie im Paradies vorkommt

Die Farben des neuen Tages verheißen eine neue
Hoffnung, denn alles, was einem nur Momente zuvor grau,
düster und ausweglos erschien, erstrahlt nun im Licht der
aufgehenden Sonne und wirkt nicht mehr bedrohlich

Man kann die Dinge im neuen Licht sehen;
neue Wege erkennen, die man vorher nicht sah
Neue Perspektiven entfalten sich vor den Augen,
die im Schatten der Nacht verborgen waren

Alles scheint auf diesen Augenblick gewartet zu haben;
auf den Sonnenaufgang - die Hoffnung eines neuen Tages!

Ein seltsamer Gedanke

Manches im Leben ist wie ein Foto,
man kann nur ein einen Teil des Ganzen sehen
einen Ausschnitt von allem, was da ist -
einen Teil der Geschichte, doch nicht den
vollständigen Roman

Wer diese "Fotos" als Außenstehender
betrachtet, hat einen anderen Blickwinkel als
die, die dabei waren und diese Momentaufnahmen
festgehalten haben

Einiges mag dem Auge des Betrachters verborgen
bleiben, die man als "Fotograf" miterlebt hat
Anderes wird erst durch einen Blick von außen
offensichtlich, weil man es beim Festhalten
des Augenblicks nicht mitbekommen hat und
oftmals, weil man das Nahe liegende nicht
sehen kann, wenn man mitten im Geschehen ist

Ab und zu kann man als "Fotograf" nur das
Abbild erkennen - das "Negativ" und
es braucht Zeit sich zum "Positiv" zu entwickeln
In einigen Fällen benötigt es jemand von außen,
der das Ganze in das richtige Licht rücken kann

Back and forth

When I told you that I love you,
I meant it - and I still do
But what is this thing now:
Soul-Bound, True Love, Obsession,
Mind-Control or Co-dependency?
I don't know it anymore
You make me lose myself
I don't know who I am anymore
All those ups and downs
Back and forth

I don't know, where this is going
I'm not sure, if you know
where this way leads to or
even who you have become
Back and forth
I cannot see whether
I'm coming or going
Nor can you

There are times, when I think
You know me better than anyone
You can understand me
You're close to me
You're by my side
Helping me through my hard times
Making me forget my tears and fears
Laugh with me in my good times
Having fun through the playfulness

Helping me heal and
Healing yourself as well by
letting me show you the
deep love I have for you
Up and down
Back and forth

Each time I think I know you
You turn it all around
Push me in some dark corner
Where I cannot see through
the shadows

Everything is the same grey mist
Everyone is a dark silhouette,
whether they're enemies or friends
No one lends me a hand
No one sheds a light in the dark

Sometimes I need to trust
the next best person and
hope that it's a friend

I come halfway through
the shadows only to see
you still there with that gleam
Back and forth

You still seem to shine
You still seem to love me
But you seem to have walls
around your heart
The shadows on your soul
prevent you to put things straight
You beckon me back
Into your world

But I fell again into the traps
around your heart
to prevent intruders
to get close to you
Back and forth

I come out of those traps hurt
Each wound gets deeper
Making my heart bleed
Making me stumble and sway

I still try to break down
the walls around your heart
But they're too strong
It all backfires to me
Making me see what a fool I am
and what a bigger fool you are
Back and forth

It seems that I act childish
when I try to reach you
while you look upon me
in that immaculate aloof style
like a perfect statue

Polished and shiny in the sun
and so untouchable and cold
So out of reach from any emotion
making me itch to throw dirt at you
To get any reaction from you
To show me your emotions
To provoke either a thunderstorm
or a breakthrough
Back and forth

Is it too much to ask of you
to come out with the truth
to draw the line
to put it straight
to let me know
where I stand in your heart.

Do you love me?
Do you hate me?
Do you even like me?
Am I something to you at all?
Am I a friend or a pal?

Am I just someone you know?
Do you care at all?
Back and forth

You made me come back
to you all the time
I always come down your way,
but darling that's not my way

If you want me in your life,
you need to come down
from your high horse
back to me at the crossing

And we create a new path together
because following one another
only makes one stumble and fall
and the other one walk alone again

None of them can listen to
The other one or see the other one
or even be there for the other one

One is fighting their way forward
and the other one is fighting to follow
It only weakens both

Only together we could be strong,
if you choose to create a path with me
Back and forth

I know I cannot force you to love me,
but you cannot force me not to love you,
even if you don't care or even hate me

My heart is still beating for you
The love inside can conquer it all
And someday it's strong
enough to let you go

So, come on, darling no more
playing hide and seek,
Tell me the truth

Be open to me and
all above to yourself!

Einbildung ist auch eine Bildung...

Mag sein, dass ich das dumme, naive Ding bin,
für das du mich immer gehalten hast,
aber das macht dich auch nicht klüger, oder?

Sonst würdest du nicht herumlungern und
den Worten eines dummen Dings Aufmerksamkeit
schenken, wenn du ganz andere Dinge tun könntest...

..wichtigere Dinge als sich mit dem Geschwafel
eines wirren Hirns auseinander zu setzen

Aber du bist hier, was eigentlich schon genug
Erklärung für dich sein sollte, wo du wirklich
stehst, wenn du ehrlich mit dir selbst bist...

Ein seltsamer Gedanke

Manchmal ist das Leben schon komisch
Viele sehen in mir einen Engel
und so mancher bezeichnet dich als Teufel

Im Alltag stellst du dich als jemand
mit einer Engelsgeduld heraus
Jemand, der Leuten Liebe, Nähe,
Geborgenheit und Gelassenheit geben kann

Mein Alltag lässt mir innerlich
die metaphorischen Teufelshörnchen wachsen
und ich werde einfach mal zur Bestie,
weil mich die Dinge aufregen, auslaugen
oder in die Enge treiben

So kann der Schein trügen und es ist besser,
wenn wir uns nie wirklich begegnen, weil ich
 dich sonst mit Sicherheit verschlingen könnte

Ist es keine Liebe..?

Du sagtest, es ist keine Liebe, weil du
keine Schmetterlinge im Bauch fühlst

Ist keine Liebe, wenn du jemand vermisst,
weil du ihn nicht täglich sehen kannst?

Ist es keine Liebe, wenn du dich danach
sehnst zu sehen oder zu hören, ob es ihm gut geht?

Ist es keine Liebe, diesen Menschen in deine Welt
zu integrieren?
Ist es keine Liebe, wenn du dir eine Welt ohne denjenigen
nicht vorstellen kannst, weil er nicht
mehr aus deiner Welt wegzudenken ist?

Ist es keine Liebe, dass du seine Nähe suchst und
ihm im Gegenzug auch Nähe bietest?

Ist es keine Liebe, wenn du die Macken
und Eigenheiten deines Gegenübers akzeptieren
kannst, ohne den anderen ändern zu wollen? Wenn
du den anderen als gleichwertigen Partner annimmst,
damit er das auch dir gegenüber spiegeln kann?

Ist es keine Liebe, wenn du dem anderen Vertrauen,
Zuneigung und Offenheit entgegen bringst, ihm deine
Stärken und Schwächen zeigst und du selbst sein kannst?

Ist es keine Liebe, wenn du für denjenigen alles tun würdest, um ihm ein gutes Gefühl, Geborgenheit und Halt zu geben?

Ist es keine Liebe, wenn du deinem Gegenüber versuchst verstehen zu geben wie viel er dir bedeutet mit allem, was du hast und geben kannst?

Ist es keine Liebe, wenn du für denjenigen um die halbe Welt reist, um bei ihm sein zu können?
Ist es keine Liebe, wenn du deinem Gegenüber auch mal seinen Freiraum geben kannst?

Ist es keine Liebe, wenn du dir denjenigen einfach nicht aus dem Kopf schlagen kannst und dir das Herz herausreißen müsstest, um das Gefühl abzustellen?

Ist es keine Liebe, wenn du für denjenigen kämpfst, um bei ihm zu sein?
Ist keine Liebe, wenn dein Herz blutet, wenn demjenigen Schmerz und Leid widerfährt?

Ist keine Liebe, wenn dir die Ohren klingeln, wenn du seinen Namen hörst?

Nicht jede Liebe braucht Schmetterlinge, manche Liebe reift langsam, manch einer schleicht sich klammheimlich in dein Herz und setzt sich da fest und du möchtest ihn gar nicht daraus verbannen - Im Gegenteil, du möchtest denjenigen nie wieder missen.

Dreams and thoughts are like stars...

They can be fleeting, short-lived,
just a twinkling that already dies down
at the end of our mind's horizon

Others are so out of reach and intangible
that you feel you never get them

Others are just cold and
turn out as gas and dust

Others are in spaces,
in which you have no air to breath
in which you're stuck
in a constant limbo and
you cannot move forward
or backward or even fly

Others are the only constant
in the chaos of your inner universe

They can show signs and images
that mark your personality
That only you and certain people
can read to guide you through your life

Others show you that even
in the darkest night there's
a light that sparkles until
the next morning

It remains night after night and
even is present in the light

The little sparks that even can
show you in a way that
there's such much out there
than you and me

They can make you believe
in the connection to other worlds
in the existing of other forms of being
in the endless possibilities of the universe

An old song that I wrote as teenager, but I felt, it needed to change a bit for this book. Though it is mostly as it was – so, yes, I wrote this way even then:

I won't cry
()- background vocals

Oohoohoohoo yeah, yeah
yeah

I.. I know the truth is hurting.. hurting
deep down to my heart
that keeps my mind in darkness
I.. I know you won't be mine…
You left me alone
You just broke my heart
My world's in pieces
(Have you ever loved me?)

But I miss you (all the time)
Now my life's lonely and cruel
(You can't stay with me like that)

Chorus:
I won't cry
I can't believe what you said
Your love passed me by
(Can't get you out of my mind)
I won't cry
It hurts me so deep
But I try to leave it all behind (Oh, oh)

I... I'm feeling lost because
my world is upside down
You seem to hide away from my love
I... I wished you could stay but
the story tells you to go

An empty space is the reminder of you
Maybe our love was only an illusion
(Growing and thriving in my mind)

Oh, I miss you (You'll never know)
And so my life's lost and gloomy
(Does it mean anything to you?)

Chorus

All I ever wanted is your love
that's why I still believe in you
(Honey, why don't you understand?)
Though your history made you harsh
My love for you is still in my heart,
mind and soul
I still can feel you by my side
If you could listen to your heart
and find the love inside
I would be yours again
(If we could believe in dreams)

Oohoohoohoo yeah, yeah

Die Magie der Musik

Die Musik brachte uns zusammen
Für einen Moment waren wir zwei Herzen,
die im Gleichklang schlugen
Zwei Seelen, die im Zauber des Augenblicks
erkannten wie sie ihre Innenwelten
teilen konnten und sie gegenseitig zurückstrahlten
Du brachtest eine Saite in mir zum klingen,
die ich nicht kannte

Mein Herz wollte nur noch dieses Lied singen,
das Ruhe in mein Chaos bringen konnte
Der Takt zweier Herzen im Einklang
der Melodie der Gefühle

Zwei Leidenschaften, die sich magisch anzogen,
um sich auszuleben und auszubalancieren
Du hast mir den Weg der Harmonie gezeigt,
den man nur als Einheit finden kann

Ich wollte an die Träume glauben,
die du in den schönsten Farben ausgemalt hast
Mein Innerstes sehnte sich nach diesen Welten,
die mich wie ein geheimnisvoller Sog
in deinen Bann zogen

Dein Charme, dein Lächeln, der Takt deines Herzens,
die Leidenschaft deiner Seele, die auf mich einwirkten,
ließen mich glauben, du würdest genauso fühlen

Die Musik ist lange verstummt und mein Herz
schlägt noch im selben Takt, doch du bist fort
Du hast mich mit dem Rausch der Gefühle
überschüttet, nur um mit einem Lächeln zu
verschwinden

Ich stehe hier immer noch mit der Hoffnung
auf die Welten, die nur du mir zeigen kannst

Ich stehe hier mit der Hoffnung,
dass du irgendwann die Träume selbst sehen
kannst, die du mir gegeben hast

Ich stehe hier mit der Hoffnung, dass du nicht nur
den Zauber des Augenblicks ausgekostet hast,
sondern dem Takt deines Herzens folgen kannst

Ich stehe hier mit der Hoffnung, dass du nicht nur
der Verlockungen der Scheinwelten nachjagst,
sondern die Melodie zweier Herzen erkennst, die
für alle Zeiten im Gleichklang schlagen können

Hallo mein Schatz!
Das Leben ist voller Entscheidungen,
dann und wann stehen wir vor neuen Wegen,
die wir mit Begleitung gehen können oder
allein gehen müssen

Wenn wir Wege allein gehen sollen,
dann scheinen diese gelegentlich länger
und dunkler als sie wirklich sind
Wir brauchen Beherztheit sie zu gehen
Diese Courage wird oft von anderen ausgetestet
und einige von ihnen treten sie mit Füßen
Mitunter scheint nichts einen Sinn zu ergeben oder
wir scheinen schwach und bedeutungslos zu sein

Aber nicht einmal Superhelden sind auf ihren
Heimatplaneten etwas Besonderes, wo
jeder diese großen Kräfte besitzt
Erst die neue Welt und die neuen Umstände
haben sie zu Superhelden gemacht

Auch ein Superheld hat seine Schwächen,
auch er braucht Leute, die ihn ein Stück weit
auf seinem Weg begleiten
Leute, die zu ihm stehen, ihn lieben und
das Beste in ihm hervorbringen

Mitunter haben wir unsere "Superkräfte"
- das Beste - in uns schlummern,
aber diese "Kräfte" können wir nicht finden,
wenn sie niemand zu brauchen scheint
Es sind Familien, Freunde, Bekannte oder Partner,
die uns diese Seite zeigen können,
indem sie das Beste in uns erwecken und
uns einfach mal ab und zu einen Spiegel vorhalten

Auch wenn diese Leute nicht immer dein Leben
lang mit dir deinen Weg gehen oder jeden Weg
mitgehen, so kannst du doch sicher sein, dass
du sie immer im Herzen mitnimmst und dass
sie auf die eine oder andere Weise bei dir sind

In stillen Momenten, wenn du in dich horchst,
kannst du sie fühlen
Egal, was noch kommt, du hast deine Familie
und Freunde an deiner Seite, selbst wenn du
sie nicht immer spürst
Leute, die dir das Beste in dir zeigen und
denen du es wieder geben kannst.

Ich bin immer für dich da,
Deine Astrid

The Dreams are gone

The Dreams are gone and
Life goes on, because it always does
Only without a sense or an aim now
I lost my Wings forever and
nothing can bring them back

I know, there are people,
who wanted to save this "little angel"
It makes sense to save
a broken, poor soul
But it's an absurd thing
to rescue the destroyer
And it's all I ever be
The Queen of demolishing

I'll destroy everything and everyone,
who tries to get me out of my hole
as I damaged my own wings over the years
I plug out the feathers - one by one
until there's nothing more -
Not even a shadow of anything
It's all beyond repair
It's not that I do it on purpose,
but it's in the way I am
I gave a lot of people the ideas of dreams,
only to disappoint them
or even hurt them in the end
with my impulsive behaviour

or with my very slow activity
or with my complicated and confusing ideas,
which all together is either upsetting
or boring to others

Even people, who rely on me
learn that I can let down without knowing
and my inept skills do the literal part
Sometimes I really have no sense at all
Often things go down the wrong way
So, I stand here naked
Stripped off the wings I tried to fly with
I know for sure that I'm not meant to fly,
because I never ever really could
though I am a dreamer

Always restrained by my own mind
and though I always wanted to soar
I only "hopped" over the mounds,
believing myself to float in the air
I was telling myself and others
that it can happen someday
It never happened and now it's too late
There are dreams that will never
come back, which is hard,
when they were all you had

People say that I'm smart and
still I feel like an idiot far too often,
because I cannot find the grip
on my thoughts and dreams,
wishes, when I need to

Everything is scattered in my brain
or lost in a mist of swirling thoughts
I know, it's all there, but I cannot reach it
I know, I lost too many chances

Now I don't know what to think anymore
I realised I cannot always trust
my senses, so I'm more confused by all
I cannot trust my feelings anymore
I lost it all, sitting in a dark hole,
I need to crawl out of it each day
Fighting every day with the chaos
to get everything in order
And it's only a matter of time
until I fall back and the hole gets deeper

So, I gave the rest of my dreams to
others, so they could fly for me
And when I didn't interfere them,
they could soar to the stars as
it never worked for me

I know, it's for the best
that I don't have any wings
Because I'm not only destroying
my dreams, but others as well
I cannot stop myself from interfere
sooner or later I hunt them all down
Yearning to get new dreams
So, my new "hobbies" are apologising
and cleaning up the mess I made

No, it's better to let this broken soul,
where she is or she'll destroy you
and that is a fact!

Of course, I still have silly ideas
Hey, I'm still a dreamer
But none of them are worth the effort
They lead nowhere and
They only make people lose
more than they had

They feel like selling their souls to me
and I'm not the devil
Just someone, who's unaware of
stealing other people's time and energy
So, waiting to get new wings for me
either by giving them to me or
growing them myself is a foolish thing to do
I only leave more ashes behind
than I already have

No, it's better for me and the world,
just to go on without them

So einen Quatsch träume ich nachts zusammen:

Ich will dich immer

Ich will dich immer und immer wieder,
selbst wenn ich mal keine Lust auf dich habe
Ich will dich immer,
selbst wenn ich dich mal hasse

Ich will dich immer,
selbst wenn du unausstehlich bist oder explodierst
Ich will dich immer,
auch wenn ich dich nicht sehen mag
oder du mir mal zuwider bist

Ich will dich immer,
auch wenn du meine Grenzen überschreitest
und selbst dann wenn du es absichtlich tust

Ich will dich immer,
mit allem, was da ist oder nicht da ist
Ich will dich immer,
auch wenn du alt und grau bist
Ich will dich immer,
auch wenn du nicht da bist

Ich will dich immer,
auch wenn du mir nicht zur Seite stehst

Ich will dich immer,
selbst mit der Dunkelheit in deiner Seele
Ich will dich immer,
weil meine Liebe zu dir größer ist als das

Ich will dich immer,
weil du der Eine und Einzige in meinem Herzen bist
Ich will dich immer,
weil du mich immer willst

Ich will dich immer,
weil du dich vor langer Zeit in deiner Seele
für mich entschieden hast

Ich will dich immer,
weil nur mit dir mein Tag heller wird
und ich Hoffnung auf mehr helle Tage habe
Ich will dich immer,
du der Richtige bist durch alle Zeiten!

AN: zum Thema "hassen", irgendwie passte "ich mag dich nicht" da nicht rein.. weil es das nicht ganz ausdrückt.. es ist mehr ein "Ich kann dich gerade nicht ausstehen"- Ding, aber das trifft es auch nicht ganz, deshalb habe ich den Ausdruck gewählt!

Manchmal reicht mir zur Inspiration ein
kleiner 3-Zeiler, den meine Nichte für mich
mit 7 verfasst hat. Ist sozusagen der Titel.

"Liebe das Herz
Es kann lieben
Das Herz ist rot"

Rot wie die Liebe
Rot wie das Blut
Manchmal blutet mein Herz
für dich und andere

Liebe das Herz
und die Seele
nicht was der Verstand diktiert
nicht das Äußere
nicht das Materielle
nicht den Status

Liebe das Herz
Es kann lieben
Alles andere ist nur
äußerer Schein
Denn nur das Herz der Dinge
ist das Wesen - die Essenz
Das, was Menschen berührt

Nur das Herz kann das
Wesentliche sehen
Nur das Herz kennt die
wirklichen Antworten
Nur das Herz erkennt
die echten Freunde
Nur das Herz erkennt
die eigentliche Familie

Schau in dein Herz
und es zeigt dir den Weg
zur einzig wahren Liebe
Folge dem Herzen und
du wirst eines finden, das im
Einklang mit deinem schlägt
Genau den Menschen,
den du "mein Herz" nennst

Vertraue deinem Herzen,
denn es kennt die Wahrheit
in dir und in anderen Menschen
Es kann dir nichts passieren,
solange du ihm traust und im
Einklang mit dir und anderen bist

Liebe das Herz
Es kann lieben
und das wahrhaft

In a fantasy world

Sometimes when I close my eyes
I drift into the twilight zone
I'm connecting to the astral level
with my soul, in which
everything seems in a dream-like state,
though I'm not dreaming

Where the spirit is close
and whispers about
soul connections and
great learning through
mutual mirroring

Where the souls are reminded
that bargains were made,
before we were born
And your soul calls out to me
It connects with mine
and be with me,
when I need it the most
or your soul needs it

Your soul's bonding with mine
and you don't even know that
in your level-headed world
A paradise, where you have all
you want, love and need
where you're safe and loved

Where you have the power
where you even have all
that matters to your heart
where your heart feels at home

Where you can trust those dear to you
where you can wrap everyone
around your finger with a smile
where lots of people try
to gain your attention and
want a piece of that world

I know, you're happy in your world
where you can live in bliss
I don't begrudge it to you
You deserve it

Your soul still bonds
with my soul nevertheless
unknown to your mind

And it seeks mine
and it helps me,
when I feel bad
and it sends me energy,
when I feel low
and it cries out to me,
when you're feeling bad,
so I can help you heal

Sometimes I can feel,
what you feel,
I can hear your voice inside me and
I can feel your hand in mine
I can see you in my head,
know what you want to say
or what you wear
before I can see you
all in my little dream-like world,
even if I'm awake

I cannot really tell you about
the exhilarating and wonderful,
deep feelings this bond can create,
It's so hard to explain, it's beyond words
It can feel warm, even hot like fire

It can feel like dancing and singing
Though those things scratch only
the surface, it's much deeper than that
It can create joy beyond anything
you can imagine with your brain

It lifts me up, when I'm close to give up
And when we visit the other body
in an astral way,
We can feel the other body as our own,
and experience what they do
It's a feeling many people yearn for

But it won't reach your mind
I know, in your world that sounds
like a fantasy or an obsession

I know, I always will have your soul
tied to mine in a deep rooted way,
no one can stop that,
but it will never enter your
level-headed world, where your mind rules

Where you live with your soul-mate
and all you want, love and need
Where you can enjoy live with all you have

I know, I ruined any chance
that you might really feel and accept
the soul connection for what it is

Now there's no place for this
humbug in your world,
because I forced with my impatience
my perception and emotions onto you

I pushed you into unknown water
and not letting you find the truth
inside yourself on your own
But I don't think that another decade
will change your mind about that view

Anyway, I would never ask you to
give up your world with
your dreams and wishes in it
I know, even if you wanted to,
you cannot give it up or
even leave it behind

You're too deep into it,
it follows you everywhere you go
and it remains when
we're not here anymore

I know, this is your world,
you chose of your own accord
you want to stay there,
where you are happy and loved
as the person you are
in the way as it should be
and the way you deserve it

I'd never take this away from you
I would never fight this
It's where you belong with your heart
I just wish you all the best and love
in your world and
I live in my own dream-like world,
with the connection to your soul

An odd creature

Someone told me
I'm acting like an odd creature
In a certain way I am an odd creature
Strange and confusing to all others
Nobody seems to know me at all

Fears and wrong information
That's what they've been told about me
And I started to run - run away from this
Running, searching, looking for you,
my friend

Do you know that you're my counterpart?
You're my twin flame - no matter what is between us
We're different - but we're still the same!
Cosmic and not to understand to normal people

I can sense what other people think about me
I'm an odd creature, it's in my nature
To perceive things in a different way
Sometimes I cry out to someone, who knows me

You're different in the way you act
But sometimes you're just like me, the weird one
You know and understand me, my friend
Let's run - run away from this
Running, searching, trying to find open minds
As long as we have each other
we get stronger every day, we two odd creatures!

A jungle of emotions

I'm tangled in a jungle of emotions
I don't know what's what anymore
Whether I'm coming or going
I cannot tell you
what I feel anymore

I got trapped in my own feelings
Learning that I can't trust
every emotion in me

Living with a distortion of
perception in a world, where
my feelings and reactions
are often not appropriate
Either too loud or too low
Either too much or too little
or even not all
Either too enthusiastic
or too harsh
Either too gentle or too rude
That confuses me even more

I don't know what to feel,
especially when I get only silence
as an answer
It makes me think that
I'm not right

I'm not like everyone else,
I never was
I don't know, if I ever will be

I know, people like to think
it's a good thing not to be
like everyone else

But when you're in love with
someone, you want the reactions
everyone else shows to you

Otherwise you have no clue,
what the other one feels
And it doesn't feel like love,
but like a survival training
getting strange reactions to your
attempts of showing your love

One thing gone down wrong
I might turn out as
beast unknowingly
The question is; is it worth
the effort to gain my attention,
living with the fear I can destroy you?
I can't answer that - only time can tell

Nachdem ich so einiges mitgekriegt habe über Vorstellungen und Erwartungen an andere Menschen, hier meine Gedanken dazu:

Regeln, um der Held meiner Träume zu sein

Die erste Regel ist,
es gibt keine Regeln, denn Helden will ich nicht

Aber der Mann meiner Träume
zu sein ist auf der einen Seite sehr einfach,
auf der anderen Seite sehr schwer

Einfach du selbst sein mit allem,
was da ist und was nicht
Ich brauche keine Shows oder
Selbstdarstellungen,
das kenne ich zur genüge
Das mag ich im Alltag nicht

Viel mehr kommst du als
"Traumprinz" bei mir rüber,
wenn du nicht auf einem
hohen Ross sitzt, sondern
wenn du auf meiner Ebene bist

Ich kann eher Leute bewundern,
die auch mal ihre Schwächen haben

Wenn du mir vertraust und dich mir
anvertrauen kannst und ich dir vertrauen kann,..

Wenn du mir das Gefühl gibst dir wertvoll
zu sein und mir die Chance gibst es dir auch zu zeigen,..

Wenn du mich nicht ständig außen vor lässt,
sondern mich ab und zu mal mit einbeziehst,
mit mir redest und dich mir zuwendest
und wenn ich im Gegenzug das Gleiche
mit dir tun kann,...

Wenn du mich sein lassen kannst wie ich bin
mit all' den Spinnereien und Macken
und Ausbrüchen und sonstigem Mist oder
zumindest versuchst mich so zu akzeptieren,
so wie ich es bei dir tun werde...

Wenn du dich aber trotzdem auch zurückziehen
kannst, weil du dich bei mir nicht einengst fühlst
und mir den gleichen Freiraum gibst...

Wenn du auch mal nichts sagen kannst
oder auch mal zu viel sagst oder dich
trotzdem bei anderen einmischen möchtest,
um zu helfen oder mal in die Luft gehst oder
oder vielleicht weinst oder Ego-Streichel-Einheiten brauchst
oder eventuelle andere Macken nicht
versteckst...

Wenn du trotz aller Spinnereien oder
seltsamen Eigenschaften bei mir nicht verstellen
musst und mir dasselbe zugestehst,...

Wenn du nicht versuchst nach deinen
Vorstellungen und Erwartungen zu formen,
genauso wie ich es nicht tue,...

Wenn ich das Gefühl habe, dass du auf meiner Seite bist
und du mich trotz allem Blödsinn noch nicht verlassen
hast, ...

...dann hast du eigentlich schon gewonnen

Natürlich werde ich nicht erwarten, dass du
mir mehr geben kannst als du bereit bist zu geben,
du gibst das, was du kannst und was du hast - nicht mehr
und nicht weniger

Und wenn du das Gleiche bei mir ertragen kannst,
dann bist du der Mann meiner Träume

A strange thought

Sometimes it seems that we fight
demons that others see as teachers
or even as salvation

But it's not easy to see the light
When you're only fighting
with no real direction or
no clue, who you can trust

When you don't know what's
worth to fight for anymore,
because many dreams and
purposes get lost on the way

When you don't have any
friends, loved ones, family
and certainly no reason to fight for
You slowly lose your strength
and your will to fight

So, if you want to see the light
you need to dream
you need a purpose
you need something
worth to fight for
Only then you can live
with all the up and downs

Zu dem Thema Held meiner Träume, noch ein englisches Möchtegern-Gedicht:

"My Super-Hero"

My "super-hero" is a man,
who has "super-powers" of his own
He knows exactly his own boundaries
and respects them

And though he's independent,
he's not afraid to ask for help
and he knows he can rely on me
as much as I can rely on him

His humanity, vulnerability, generosity
gentleness and love are his shield and power
I can follow his lead if I need to,
as well as he can follow me

Sometimes he needs to be rescued by me,
as much as he can safe me from the traps I fell in

He doesn't need anything to impress me
or to act in a way society dictates

He can be himself around me
He knows that not all that glitters is gold
and see the true substance in life

I can the stars in his eyes and
his smile brings light to my heart

He can bring me the sweetest dreams,
in which we can fly through the universe
in all kind of ways

We can share our passions in all we do
and still have our freedom

He's my home, where I can belong
where I feel safe, peaceful, loved,
comfortable and accepted
Where I feel content and happy in my own skin,
just as he's feeling I'm the one he can home to,
the one that can put him at ease,
the one with whom he can feel secure in his own skin

I can make his dreams come true,
if he believes in me as I do believe in him
We teach each other all we need to know and more

He's my true love and I'm his true love
as we mirror all there is
He's everything to me just as I am his world!

If I was the one

If I was the one
You could dream of
You would never need anybody else
You always could rely on me
My heart would be your home
I would be everything you need

If I was the one
You could see
I would be perfect just for you
I would show you the beauty
no one else can see
Only you'd know me as a whole
as I would know you as well
Not fragments of certain displays

If I was the one
You could love
I would show your own sweetness
that you seem to forget
I would bring out your tenderness
and sensitivity, which you mask
I remind you of the loveable being
inside that you lost over the years
Maybe I could show you a bit of heaven

If I was the one
You could hold dear
I would remind you that you
can be loved for just being yourself

I would be the one by
your side no matter what
No outside circumstance like
old age, sickness or poverty or
such things change that
I love you and I always will

But you see me only as
a source of irritation
for your peaceful life
Someone, who's getting on
your nerves just to get
your attention
Someone in the crowd

I just wished
I had the chance to be the one
But all of this needs to be
a dream right now
There are too many obstacles
in the way

Obstacles I can't overcome all alone
And you have no clue
I don't want to bother you with
My foolish feelings
Everything's as it was and
I will never be the one

The boy inside

I know that you don't want me
to behave "so childishly"
Maybe you want me to "grow up"
Perhaps I will grow,
though I don't think
I can be the way
you wish me to be

It make me sad, you even cannot
see the boy inside you anymore!
I can see that sweet, little chap
gleaming out of your eyes with
mirth each time you laugh
I notice the mischief,
when I read between the lines
of your behaviour sometimes

I know that you hide still some
silly, childish and fantastic ideas
underneath your cool exterior
I know that you still follow
your lofty dreams
though they're masked behind
your calculated demeanour
I realised that you even have
the ability to see things in
a childlike wonder, but you
forbid yourself that adventures

I can see that little boy inside you
wants to come out and play,
but you locked him away

So, this is what is be grown-up -
to keep a part of you locked away?!

I know, it's not always fun and
games in this world

But you can take the youthful,
happy and easy way each time
the seriousness and harshness
overshadows your love and life

Joy and adventures are sometimes
essential to keep the balance
Sometimes you can find wonders
in doing silly things

Just let the little boy inside you
come out and play every
now and then!

Die zwei Furien

Die verlorenen Furien hatten
Gerechtigkeit gefordert
Die Ruhmeshalle der sanften
Helden blieb ihnen verschlossen

Hier standen sie nun erzürnt
und voller Seelenqual
Das Chaos in ihnen und
um sie schien ausweglos
Sollte dies nun das Ende einer
tiefen Liebe sein?

Nur das strahlende Mondlicht
brachte Ruhe und Abkühlung
Die glitzernden Sterne
brachten ihnen Zuversicht
Weise Seelen erzählten von
Zeichen der Hoffnung:
Federn, Münzen und
Sternschnuppen sollten den
rechten Weg weisen

Die eine Furie folgte der
richtigen Sternschnuppe
Sie fand den Weg zurück
zum sanften Helden und
wurde wieder die großherzige
Göttin von einst

Die andere verlorene Furie
wurde von Zeichen überhäuft
Massenhafte Federn,
Münzen und Sternschnuppen
schürten zu viele Hoffnungen
Leider entpuppte sich jeder neue
Weg als Sackgasse

Die verlorene Furie hat sich
immer mehr in eine verwirrte,
frustrierte, alte Hexe verwandelt

Jetzt einen Weg durch das Chaos
zu finden erscheint fast unmöglich
Selbst wenn die verstörte Hexe
einen Weg findet, scheint die
Verwandlung zur liebenswerten
Göttin nahezu undenkbar

Vielleicht würde der sanfte
Held bei ihr zum
verdrehten Hexenmeister
Vielleicht wäre es besser
die kauzige Hexe ziehen zu lassen
Vielleicht könnten sich die
beiden auch gegenseitig heilen
und gestärkt gemeinsam
in eine Zukunft gehen

Das Ende ist offen -
Liebe oder nicht -
Alles ist möglich!

You took your love away

You took your love away
I'm too dull to feel anymore now
You cut off your soul like a
lightning from a clear blue sky
You took my love with it
I sensed the metaphorical cut
right in my fingers,
when you did it

My fingers were burning,
feeling that the thrilling,
exhilarating, all-consuming,
tingling, satisfying, warming,
pulsating and electrifying
calming, heartfelt
and peaceful sensation
flowing out of me fast,
when I was losing
the touch of your soul
It left me cold, disheartened
and lethargic in my body
I'm like an empty shell now

Hardly keep my things together
I have no idea what to do
No emotion to keep me going
I feel like blind to feelings now

I lost a love too big, too deep
and too strong for words
Actually it's a love that even
couldn't really be broken

 - It's still there -

Buried deep within and
locked away in fear
It seems that you got scared
by this kind of love so
powerful, so overwhelming

Some people cannot
comprehend and even
cannot stand this sort of love,
even if they wish for it
even if they long for it
even if they search for it
even if they yearn for it

When they have it
It's too much to bear for them
and they can't accept it
they run away,
because it takes courage
to love this much

Now I'm all alone,
stripped off that love

I don't know
what I should feel
There is this hole in me,
which cannot be filled
by anyone but you

No one else can give
me this unique love
but you took it away
Leaving my heart to bleed

It seems you weren't
ready for this love
And all I can do is wait
for things to change
one way or another!

Liebe berechnen? (Meine Sicht)

Ich habe gelesen, dass man
immer mehr Gefühle mit dem
Computer erkennen kann
Die Frage kam auf, ob man Liebe
berechnen kann
In meinen Augen bleibt aber der
"menschliche Faktor" nicht berechnet

Solange es Momente gibt, in denen
man dem Traumpartner wie aus
heiterem Himmel trifft, solange ist
die Liebe nicht zu berechnen
Sicher, man kann bio-chemische
und körperliche Reaktionen messen,
die man bei Liebe zeigt

Aber man kann noch so viele
übereinstimmende Faktoren auf
einen potentiellen Partner berechnen
und trotzdem kann es auch mal nicht
"der/die Richtige" sein
Oft genug sind die richtigen Partner
genau die, von denen wir es selbst
am wenigsten erwartet haben

Wenn uns ein Mensch verzaubern kann,
dann man es nicht berechnen -
es geschieht einfach
und das ist die Magie der Liebe!

More than that

They say, you want to impress me
I only saw you strutting around
like a proud peacock
Smug was what your smile
appeared to be

You try to hide your flaws
behind that exalted behaviour
to show me a perfect stature
I don't need any Show-Offs
I need more than that

They say, you move the stars for me
I only saw you putting effort in
all of your own dreams without
taking mine into consideration
You only fly in your own sky
where I cannot always follow
Flying like an eagle and
leaving me to feel like
a penguin trying to fly

You try to show me
how to reach lofty goals
in the way you do
But that isn't my way
I need more than that

They say, you would do
anything for me
I only saw you making
your own life wonderful
without thinking of me
You merely steamrolled me
with what you have and
with what you exhibit and
with your cool demeanour

You only wanted to show me
what you can give me and
what you can be for me
I don't care for the prestige
I need more than that

I don't want you to change
I need the real person underneath
the layers of your poise
I need your vulnerability just as
your strength and protection

I need your inability to say or
do certain things just as
your capability for saying and
doing the things that matter
I need your flaws and problems
as well as your perfect stature

I need your dreams and fantasies
just as your level-headed mind
I need your love and care
just as your calculated attitude

I need you to be a safe place
and a shoulder to cry on
as long as you let me be
the same for you
You can only impress me,
if you let me be all the
things for you that
you want to be for me

If you want to be my champion,
then accept me as
your heroine as well
If you want me to dream of you
Then let us dream together
The dreams only get bigger,
better and the most beautiful
with both of us in it

If you want to grant me wishes,
open your arms to receive
the ones I want to fulfil
If you want to impress me,
just let me impress you!

Manchmal kann man keine Worte finden

Als Menschen brauchen wir physischen Kontakt,
als einen Halt, Zuneigung, Zusammenhalt
oder einfach die Nähe zum anderen Menschen
Manchmal benötigen wir eine körperliche
Verbindung oder Bestätigung, wo uns
die Worte fehlen

Eine Umarmung, ein Streicheln,
eine Hand auf der Schulter oder auf dem
Rücken oder in der anderen Hand,
ein Kuss und noch vieles mehr -

All das kann man ohne Worte ausdrücken,
um eine Liebe, einen Zusammenhalt, eine
Verbindung zur Familie oder einer Freundschaft
zu zeigen oder gar zu bekräftigen

Ein alter Song, etwas umgeschrieben, da es nicht mehr ganz so passte... - Okay, immer noch sehr lang...

You saved my heart

1) As I ran along the crowded streets
   My body was on autopilot
   All I could do was
   Keeping the remains together
   Having no life at all
   Barely existing in a blank state
   The hell I've been put through
   Was a creation of my own mind
   Tears of depression ran down my cheeks
   I felt alone in a world full of people
   That was, when you found me
   You built a bridge to my heart in an instant
   One look of you and I felt sheltered

Chorus
   I know from the moment I met you
   You saved my heart without further ado
   Being there, when I needed someone
   You made my soul complete
   I can rely on you no matter when
   Your love is in every part of me
   I feel it deep within
   You saved my heart and my life
   Just by awakening my heart
   And loving me as I am
   I feel the love grows stronger each day

2) Before you turned up in my life
   All days were sinister and cruel
   Leaving no hope for better times
   I had no will to survive
   Only my instincts let me go on
   There's no direction without love
   When you found me, the gleam
   of hope touched my soul
   It reached deep down and
   Guided me to the light of your heart

   You melted the pain inside of me
   You're my guardian angel
   I can turn to you for everything
   You give me the love, faith and
   The strength I need to go on

Chorus
   I know from the moment I met you
   You saved my heart without further ado
   Being there, when I needed someone
   You made my soul complete
   I can rely on you no matter when
   Your love is in every part of me
   I feel it deep within
   You saved my heart and my life
   Just by awakening my heart
   And loving me as I am
   I feel the love grows stronger each day

Bridge
   I can trust you
   I can believe in you
   You bring the light into my darkness
   With you I have hope for another day
   I can feel my belief in a better world
   Coming back with your love

Chorus
   I know from the moment I met you
   You saved my heart without further ado
   Being there, when I needed someone
   You made my soul complete
   I can rely on you no matter when
   Your love is in every part of me
   I feel it deep within everywhere I go
   You saved my heart and my life
   Just by awakening my heart
   And loving me as I am
   I feel the love grows stronger each day

Ja, ich weiß, meine Songs klappen nur im Kopf. Die kann man nicht so singen.

Ein dummer Gedanke

Manchmal wünschte ich,
ich könnte echt etwas bewegen;
die Leute erreichen; auf mehr
als nur einem Wege

Ich wünschte, ich könnte
für die Leute wirklich da sein
und nicht nur mit Worten

Aber eins ums andere Mal
sind mir die Hände gebunden
und ich kann nur mit Worten
für andere da sein

Ich wünschte, dass es jemand
wirklich helfen könnte meine
wirren Gedanken zu lesen, wenn
man sich vielleicht auf die eine
oder andere Weise angesprochen
fühlen kann, aber das ist nur
ein dummer Gedanke!

I can see you

I can see you
Trying to hide your emotions
I can see you
Ignoring the world outside
I can feel you
Shutting everyone out
I can feel you
Brooding over your problems
I know you
Sort everything out for yourself
It makes me want to cry, run to you
and talk to you and hug you
But I know, you don't want me to

Maybe you don't realise anymore
that I'm here for you all the time
Maybe you take me for granted
Maybe you think I'm a babbling fool

Don't you know that I can listen silently?
Don't you know that you can cry
on my shoulder without fear of
any silly remark or ill will?
Don't you know that you still
remain my hero afterwards?
Don't you know that you are
still a strong person to me,
even if you break down?

I'm not like anyone else
I don't judge you for being weak
If you need someone to shout at
or someone to hug
or someone to talk to
or someone to hide behind
or someone just to be there
I'm here for you all the time!

I don't want to you force into
doing anything you don't want or
anything you are not ready for

Just remember, you can ask me
for help any time - even at night!
And if you cannot ask me, then
send me a sign or write letters
to me, if you need to or call me
and talk my ears off, if you must!

You know, where to find me!

Sacred places

There are places in the world
That we consider as sacred
Where we feel a certain kind of power

Where we feel calm and secure
Where we can retreat from the chaos
And hectic of our daily grind

Where we feel at home
Where we feel whole
Where we feel the need to reflect
Our lives

Where we can see the beauty in
Everything and everyone

You can find those places in nature,
it's where you initially feel drawn to
You can create those places
Everywhere you need to

You can light a candle,
Seeing it shine with power in the dark
You feel the peace of the moment

You can find that place in your heart,
when you remember the happy
moments in your life

The love you give and receive,
where your heart was shining
like a bright star

You can take those places in your
Heart everywhere and create them
Again and form new ones!

And the beauty in this is:
You can bring this place in your heart
To everyone in need of love,
light and shelter!

A sad thought

Someday my foolish heart will learn
that we were never meant to be

You never see anything in me
other than being a silly, brash person

You simply kept your distance
and remain aloof and silent

I only wanted you to notice me,
which makes me the beast in this,
who stalks the nice, shy guy

I never wanted to hurt you,
but we seem to have a habit getting
hold of the wrong end of the stick

You only seem frosty towards me
and you could never see past
the mindless, foolish, brash oaf,
who annoys you

You only get your defences up,
but sometimes you need
to keep tabs on me
Do you think I get out of control?
Or do you fear my power?

Do you fear that I put some kind
of spell on you to make do things?

What kind of spell that may be,
it only leaves me out there alone in
the rain, while you walk in the sunshine?

I never really stepped on your toes,
you always have the freedom
and the choice what to do

The only thing that has captured you
is my heart - no, that's a lie
You're in my mind, heart and soul

But one day, my foolish feelings
can catch up with what
my brain knew all along:
we were never meant to be

In den Klauen des Drachen

Wie fühlt es sich an,
wenn du in den Klauen des
Drachen steckst -
einer omnipräsenten und
omnipotenten Kreatur?

Ein Wesen, das dich mit
einem Hauch verbrennen kann?

Ein Wesen, das unverwundbar
und unangreifbar zu sein scheint?

Ein Wesen, das dich mit seinem schier
unendlichen Wissen überschüttet?

Ein Wesen, das scheinbar überall ist
und nirgends?

Es ist ein höllisches Gefühl dieser
Kreatur auf Gedeih und Verderb
ausgeliefert zu sein
Es ist aufregend, anstrengend
und erschreckend zugleich
Es ist Nichts für schwache Nerven

Doch warum suchst du dann immer
wieder die Höhle, in der sich der
Drache zurückzieht?

Du provozierst ihn, um zu sehen,
ob er dich in Flammen aufgehen lässt
oder ob du ihn besiegen kannst

Oder du willst etwas von ihm,
das dir seine Magie einverleibt und
dir somit ewiges Leben und Ruhm bringt

Oder du suchst den goldenen Drachen,
der liebenswürdig seine Weisheiten, sein
Glück und seine Kraft teilt

Was auch immer dein Beweggrund sein
mag, du hast dich in die Klauen des
Drachen begeben und nun ist es an
ihm dein Schicksal zu besiegeln!

I had this in mind, when I thought about the
meanings of my name, listening to a certain song
and things I heard over the time one way or another:

A very strange thought

Coming from somewhere outer space
Falling down to the ground with a thud
and my face smacked in the dirt
My brain's whirling from the impact
Everything seems to reel
I don't know where I am
I don't recall who I am
This doesn't feel right
This doesn't feel real
Everything feels like swimming

They say that I'm not from here
I'm not like anyone else
They say it's in my name
They say I'm from the stars
Maybe I'm a shining star
Maybe I'm a horsewoman for the gods
Maybe I'm a peaceful eagle
They say it's in the way I am
Maybe I'm an avenging angel
Maybe I'm a goddess of strife
I don't know

They say it's in the way I talk
No one seems to understand a word
I say and sometimes
I can hardly understand them

They say I can make people
do what I want
Well, that sounds like I am
a kind of master manipulator
Funny that it feels to me that
I have to run for miles from
one to another person
to get anything
And in the end it's not even
a scratch of what I asked for

They say I can talk to people
telepathically and connect to them
They say I can send my energy
to people to heal them
They say I have visions and
premonitions of what can be
Maybe I feel sometimes strangely
connected to other people
I deeply care for and having
a sense of being alerted in
potential risky moments
But that's called instinct

They say I have connections
to other dimensions and worlds
Having weird dreams
that can come true making
me just a creative being
It's all a matter of perspective

But one thing is for sure,
I feel alone in the way I am
Nobody to share my sentiments
No one here to understand me

Seems I'm really from somewhere
so out of space that
I feel alienated from everyone

Maybe I find someday a way
to fit in somehow and someone,
who understands me in some way,
but that's written in the stars!

Ich sah neulich in einem Fenster
ein Herz aus Stahl und dachte so bei mir:

Ein Herz aus Stahl hat
einige Vorteile
Es rostet nicht
Man kann auf ihm herumtrampeln
Man kann es fallen lassen
Es nimmt keinen Schaden
Es kann ewig leben!

Nur kann solch ein Herz fast nichts
erschüttern und somit leider auch
nichts im Inneren berühren

Es kann nie wirklich leben - es existiert
Es kann nie den Sonnschein in sich
aufnehmen oder sich für etwas
oder jemand wirklich erwärmen

Nur ein Feuer heißer als die Hölle kann
es zum Schmelzen bringen und dann
ist es auf ewig in der Hitze verloren

My King of Hearts

You're my King of Hearts
You always give me sensible advices
You're my mentor and my lover
You're full of adventures and spark,
excitement that inspires me
Living my live together with you
in the most happy and fulfilled way

You're my King of Hearts
You're my best friend
You're playful and mature - all in one
You guide my ways calm and gentle
You love me unconditionally
You showed me how to reach my
goals, dreams and keep my beliefs
You taught me to grow spiritually
and emotionally

I've learned my lessons well
So I will be your Queen of Hearts forever
and return everything to the sender

Als ich dir sagte...

Als ich dir sagte,
ich will dein Bestes war
nicht die Rede von Geld
oder dass ich es will

Ich will das Beste für dich
und das Beste,
was du geben kannst
und der Beste,
der du sein kannst,
ohne dich zu verbiegen

Ich will dein Bestes,
Deine Liebe für dich und
mich, so wie du sie geben
kannst - nicht mehr und
nicht weniger

Denn so klein das Beste
in dir auch zu sein scheint,
wenn du es teilst wird es
größer als du denkst
Ich will dein Bestes -
Deine Liebe!

Der äußere Schein

Nicht jeder, der uns unhöflich begegnet,
ist es auch mit Absicht, vielleicht er
Probleme und Sorgen, die er für sich behält

Jemand, der uns verwirrt erscheint,
ist vielleicht mit dem halben Herzen
bei der Sache, weil ihn leidvolle
Gedanken plagen

In vielen Fällen können gut gemeinte
Ratschläge oder Versuche der
Aufmunterung einfach mal verletzen
oder gar quälen

Rücksichtnahme ist das Wichtigste
in dem Moment, auch Sensibiltät
ist gefordert, so dass man den Rückzug
des anderen akzeptieren kann
ohne einzugreifen

Man sollte sich möglichst nur
einmischen oder Hilfe anbieten,
wenn es der andere es will

Oft genug wollen wir helfen,
aber das geht leider auch mal
den falschen Hals herunter, weil
wir nicht genau Bescheid wissen

Wir handeln dann vorschnell
und vielleicht auch falsch

Auch wenn es schwer fällt,
lieber warten und schauen,
ob der andere unsere Hilfe
will und braucht als dem
anderen noch mehr Sorgen
durch unüberlegtes Handeln
bereiten!

Music

Music reaches beyond my world
I always tried to explain what
music means to me
to put into words
to tell people what I feel

But no word can be formed
in my head to express it
Because music touches a side of
me, which runs deep down to my soul

Many people tell me
music means much to them
I know, they think it's same for me,
when I say it, but it's not

Of course, music means mucht to me,
but it's different to me
It doesn't even scratch the surface
of what I feel in every fibre of being

Nothing stops the music for me,
if there was no music in the world
or if I were deaf or out of my head
I would still sing my heart out,
though I even can't sing at all

I would still play my music,
though I even can't play
an instrument
It's all in my body;
in my heart, mind and soul

It makes me sad not to
share my music with anyone
It feels like a part of me dies
and it does

Sometimes I want to sing
my heart out to anyone
to share my sentiments
Sometimes music helps
in my darkest moments,
when nothing else can do so
and makes me go on

It's my connection to
my soul and other
people's souls

It's important to me
in every way,
because when I feel
lost and lonely,
the music can bring back
every good thing in my life

Pfeile

Wir verschießen Pfeile,
um etwas oder jemand zu treffen
Pfeile, die durch die Luft surren
und den Weg zum Ziel zeigen
Pfeile, die gemacht wurden,
um ins Schwarze zu treffen

Je nach dem, was wir treffen
wollen, richtet sich unser
Augenmerk und unsere
Konzentration auf das
gerichtete Ziel

Nur allzu oft im Leben sind
es die metaphorischen Pfeile,
die Menschen auf die eine oder
andere Art treffen sollen

Pfeile, die das Herz treffen
können die Menschen mit ihren
scharfen Spitzen stechen oder sie
werden von ihrer Magie berührt,
wenn es Amors Pfeile sind
Auf jeden Fall werden diese
Pfeile das Leben verändern

Nicht immer können wir
das Ziel klar erkennen und
wir müssen unserem Instinkt
trauen, damit wir ins Schwarze
zu treffen
Da heißt es Bogen spannen,
Augen schließen, durchatmen
und darauf vertrauen, dass
die Pfeile ans Ziel gelangen

Manchmal ist auch das
pure Glück, das einem hilft
seinen Ziel zu treffen, denn
so gut man auch ist, es gibt
immer wieder Umstände,
die einen geraden Flug
eines Pfeils verhindern

Da hilft auch nicht immer
die Erfahrung, wenn das
passiert - da kann man nur
eines tun - hoffen!
Und manch ein verloren
geglaubter Pfeil trifft sein
Ziel auf wundersamen Wege
später mitten in Schwarze
und man hat plötzlich etwas
gewonnen, mit dem man
nicht mehr gerechnet hat

Dream Lover

There was a time,
when I needed someone
You were there for me
granting every wish and dream
You are like nobody else in
this world, because you're
in a different kind of sphere
in the way you are!

When you are not near me,
I still feel no kind of fear
Because I always have you
on my mind everywhere I go
Each time I hug my pillow,
there's not a long way to you
I love you in my dreams
With you in my fantasy,
I'll never feel alone,
my Dream Lover and
That's all I need to know

Our spirits are melt together
as one and we connect in mind
Your eyes are piercing my soul,
I feel completely bared under
your knowing eyes
The eyes ablaze with fire,
though I still can feel the
devotion deep within

Though your smug smile can
freeze the hell over,
my love for you still magnifies
Though your love can be
destroying to my sanity
It certainly defies rationality,
my heart doesn't slow
I love you in my dreams
With you in my fantasy,
I'll never feel alone,
my Dream Lover and
That's all I need to know

Whenever I feel sad or lost,
You're there for me
You take away the fear and pain
with a flash of your warm smile
The thought of you is enough
to keep my sorrows at bay
And though you're not there
in flesh and blood,
I still feel your presence here
I don't care, if the sun never
shines again and night rules
forever more
You're my shining light that
guides me through the dark,
my Dream Lover
I'm sure, someday we
can see eye to eye somehow
and we will know instantly,
we are meant to be!

Danksagung

Vielen Dank an alle, die mich inspiriert haben - auf die eine oder andere Weise, bewusst oder unbewusst, ungewollt oder nicht, direkt oder indirekt, positiv wie negativ, ich danke Euch von Herzen dafür. Danke an alle Musiker, die mit ihren Songs mir eins ums andere Mal geholfen haben. Beim Schreiben höre ich nur meine Lieblingslieder!

Danke an die Leute, die sich bis zur letzten Seite durch meine wirren Gedanken gekämpft haben, jetzt habt ihr es wirklich geschafft.. mehr wird es aus dieser Reihe nicht geben. (Zumindest nicht einfach so, aber man soll niemals nie sagen..)

Zum Schluss noch vielen Dank an meine Familie und meine Freunde und Online-Kumpel, die tatsächlich direkten Einfluss auf ein paar Werke haben, auch wenn man sich nicht immer versteht, wir können trotzdem zusammenhalten.

Ein ganz besonderer Dank gilt meiner Nichte, ohne sie würde dieses Buch nicht existieren!

Auch wenn es nicht so geworden ist und sich Dinge auf die eine andere Weise ähneln beziehungsweise wiederholen, habe ich sie und ein paar andere Leute über gewisse Gedanken lächeln sehen und das war es wert.
Alles Liebe und Gute Euch allen!

Eure Astrid